THIS BOOK BELONGS TO

The Adventures of

Bella & Harry

Let's Visit Maui!

Written By

Lisa Manzione

Illustrated By

Kristine Lucco

Bella & Harry, LLC

www.BellaAndHarry.com
email: BellaAndHarryGo@aol.com

Aloha, friends!
Welcome to Maui! We have
a busy week of fun planned,
so put on your sneakers!
Here we go!

Today we are traveling
on the famous "Road to Hana",
or the "Hana Highway".

First stop...
the famous Wailua Falls.

This waterfall is over 80 feet tall
.... or about eight average sized
dolphins, from nose to tail fin!

7

"Bella, are there a lot of waterfalls on the island of Maui?"

"Yes, there are. Did you know the rain helps to keep the water flowing through the waterfalls? Plus, the moisture created from Haleakala National Park helps keep the water flowing too."

"Haleakala?"

Bella, are you speaking English? I don't understand the word you are saying."

"Well, Harry, the word 'Haleakala' is from the Hawaiian language and means 'House of the Sun'. The Hawaiian language is a Polynesian language. Both English and Hawaiian are the official languages of the state of Hawaii."

Ni'ihau

Kaua'i

O'ahu

PACIFIC OCEAN

N

W

E

S

Let's look at our map before we continue our family tour.

Hawaii

has eight main islands...
Maui, O'ahu, Kaua'i,
Moloka'i, Lana'i, Ni'ihau,
Kaho'olawe, and Hawai'i.

The islands are located in the Pacific Ocean. Maui is the second largest island in the chain.

Moloka'i

Maui

Lana'i

Kaho'olawe

The Big Island of Hawai'i

Our next stop is the Honokalani Black Sand Beach!

"Bella, I have never heard of a black sand beach before.
Why is the sand black?"

"Black sand beaches were formed when the lava from
an active volcano and the ocean water came together.
Let's touch the black sand! It feels like small, smooth pebbles."

12

"Come on Harry! We are going to hike to the lava tunnel! The lava tunnel was formed just like the black sand beach. The lava was very hot and when it mixed with the ocean water, it turned to rock."

"**This** is fun! I have never been in a lava tunnel before! Hey Bella, can we jump in the water?"

"Not here, Harry. The ocean current can be very strong in Maui. It is best to swim near a lifeguard on duty. We will go for a swim later. Now we are off to see a dormant volcano!"

"A volcano!!!"

"**Yes**, Harry. Haleakala Volcano, or the East Maui Volcano, is the world's largest dormant volcano. Dormant means the volcano is sleeping right now. The volcano has not erupted in a long time, about two hundred years ago, say most people."

"**We** are at Haleakala! Look at that huge hole in the ground!"

"Harry, that is the Haleakala Crater. It is about three thousand feet deep. The land is still very bare, with just a few plants growing. Harry? Harry!"

Oh no! Harry is chasing birds again!

"Harry, you cannot chase the birds in Maui! Those are Hawaiian geese, called 'Nene'. They are the rarest form of geese in the world!"

"Really? I almost got one!"

"Let's go Harry!!!"

NOW that we have arrived at our hotel in Wailea, we are heading down to the beach for an evening of fun! Come on, let's go!

19

"**Bella**, look over there, what are they doing?
It looks like fun!"

"**Harry**, those are 'hula' dancers. The 'hula' is more than a dance. It is the art of moving your hips and hands together in a smooth motion, telling a story. The 'hula' also includes a song or chant.

'Hula' dancers usually wear a 'lei' (a necklace made of flowers) around their neck and a grass (or 'raffia') skirt around their body."

"The sun is setting, Bella.
Our family is heading to a 'luau'.
Let's go! I am hungry!"

"Harry, how do you know there will be food at the 'luau'?"

"**Well** Bella, I have been reading about 'luaus'. A 'luau' is a traditional Hawaiian feast or party. We will be trying some local food such as poi (taro root that is boiled and then pounded), poke (raw seasoned seafood), lomi lomi salmon (salmon, tomato and Maui onion), Kalua pork and haupia (coconut pudding) for dessert. There is also a lot of fruit such as pineapples, papayas, mangos, lychees and coconuts!"

"This is so much FUN! Look over there Harry!
I see dancers and they are dancing with FIRE!"

"Yes, Bella, it is called the Samoan Fire Knife dance.
The dance dates back hundreds of years. The warriors
in Samoa (another Polynesian island) would do this dance
to show how strong they were."

"Harry, I am having so much FUN! I had no idea you knew so much about 'luaus'!"

25

Today our tour is taking us to another island. We are going with our family to the largest of the islands, the island of Hawaii.

We will have to take a quick plane ride from Kahului, Maui to Hilo, Hawaii. Once we arrive in Hilo, we are going to take a helicopter ride to see an active volcano! We will be able to see lava flowing when we fly over Hawaii Volcanoes National Park.

"**I** have never been in a helicopter before Bella, have you?"

"Yes, I have Harry. We must wear our seat belts. We also must wear headphones (with microphones) so we can stay in touch with everybody (especially the pilot). Helicopters are very noisy inside the seating area."

"**Look** Harry! The hot lava is pouring into the ocean! As the lava pours into the ocean, islands are formed. It takes millions of years, but one day this island might be larger, due to the lava flow."

"**Bella**, what is all of that smoke from?"

"Actually that is steam from the hot lava mixing with the cool ocean water, not smoke."

29

"**Bella**, the view from the helicopter is great! We can see waterfalls, volcano craters and the pretty Hawaiian coastline."

"Yes, Harry, Hawaii is very beautiful!"

We had a great time visiting the islands of Hawaii. Harry and I are back in Wailea, Maui now and are going to spend a few more days at the beach relaxing with our family. We hope you will join us on our next adventure but for now it is "aloha", or good-bye, from Bella Boo and Harry too!

Our Adventure to Maui

Bella and Harry visit a coffee bean farm.

Bella in a typical Hawiian outfit (muumuu and a lei).

Harry learning to surf.

Bella and Harry go to a pineapple plantation.

Fun Hawaiian
Words and Phrases

Aloha – Hello or good-bye

'Ae – Yes

A'ole – No

Aloha kakahiaka – Good morning

Aloha 'auinalā – Good afternoon

Aloha ahiahi – Good evening

Mahalo – Thank you

A'ole pilikia – You're welcome

Library of Congress Cataloging-in-Publications Data is available

Manzione, Lisa

The Adventures of Bella & Harry: Let's Visit Maui!

ISBN: 978-1-937616-52-6

First Edition

Book Twelve of Bella & Harry Series

For further information please visit:

www.BellaAndHarry.com

or

Email: BellaAndHarryGo@aol.com

Printed in the United States of America

Phoenix Color, Hagerstown, Maryland

April 2014

14 4 12 PC 1 1